The Literary Conference

D1571752

The Literary Conference

·

CÉSAR AIRA

Translated by Katherine Silver

A NEW DIRECTIONS PEARL

Copyright © 2006 by César Aira
Translation copyright © 2010 by Katherine Silver
Originally published by Ediciones ERA, Argentina, as *El congreso de literatura*
    in 2006; published in conjunction with the literary Agency Michael Gaeb /
    Berlin

All rights reserved. Except for brief passages quoted in a newspaper, magazine,
    radio, or television review, no part of this book may be reproduced in any form
    or by any means, electronic or mechanical, including photocopying and record-
    ing, or by any information storage and retrieval system, without permission in
    writing from the Publisher.

Manufactured in the United States of America
New Directions Books are printed on acid-free paper.
First published as a Pearl (NDP1173) by New Directions in 2010
Published simultaneously in Canada by Penguin Books Canada Limited
Design by Erik Rieselbach

Library of Congress Cataloging-in-Publication Data

Aira, César, 1949 –
    [Congreso de literatura. English]
The literary conference / César Aira ; translated from the Spanish by Katherine
    Silver.
    p. cm.
"Originally published by Ediciones ERA, Argentina, as El congreso de literatura
    in 2006"—T.p. verso.
"A New Directions Paperbook Original NDP1173"—T.p. verso.
ISBN-13: 978-0-8112-1878-8 (pbk. : alk. paper)
ISBN-10: 0-8112-1878-3 (pbk. : alk. paper)
I. Silver, Katherine. II. Title.
PQ7798.1.I7C66513 2010
863'.64—dc22

                        2009045914

10 9 8 7 6 5 4 3 2 1

New Directions Books are published for James Laughlin
by New Directions Publishing Corporation
80 Eighth Avenue, New York, NY 10011

THE LITERARY CONFERENCE

PART I

The Macuto Line

ON A RECENT trip to Venezuela I had the opportunity to admire the famous "Hilo de Macuto" or "The Macuto Line," one of the wonders of the New World—a legacy left by anonymous pirates, a tourist attraction, and an unsolved enigma. A strange monument to human ingenuity that remained a mystery for centuries and, in the process, became an integral part of a Nature that at those latitudes is as rich as all the innovations to which She gives rise. Macuto itself is one of several coastal towns spread out at the foot of Caracas and adjacent to Maiquetía, where the airport I landed in is situated. They put me up temporarily at Las Quince Letras, the modern hotel built on the beach in front of the bar and restaurant of the same name. My room faced the sea, the enormous yet intimate Caribbean Sea, blue and brilliant. The "Line" passed a hundred yards in front of the hotel; I caught a glimpse of it from my window, then went out to take a closer look.

Throughout my childhood, I, like every child of the Americas, indulged in vain speculations about the Macuto Line, a living relic through which the fictional world of pirates became real and tangible. Encyclopedias—mine was *A Childhood Treasury,* which didn't deserve its name except in those pages—contained diagrams and photographs, which I reproduced in my notebooks. And in my

5

games I would untie the knot, reveal the secret … Much later, I watched documentaries about the Line on television; I bought books on the subject and came across it many times during my studies of Venezuelan and Caribbean literature, where it appears as a leitmotif. I also followed, along with everyone else (though without any special interest), newspaper articles about new theories, new attempts to solve the enigma … The fact that new ones were continually cropping up was a clear indication that the previous ones had failed.

According to the age-old legend, the Line was devised to recover a treasure from the deep sea, a haul of immense value placed there by pirates. One of the pirates (none of the chronicles and archives used in the research identified him by name) must have been an artistic-scientific genius of the first order, a shipboard Leonardo, to have invented such a marvelous instrument that could both hide and recover the loot.

The apparatus was ingeniously simple. It was, as the name states, a line, a single line, in reality, a rope made of natural fibers stretched about three yards above the surface of the water over a marine basin off the Macuto coast. One end of the rope disappeared into the basin, then reappeared when it passed through a naturally occurring stone sheave in a rock that rose above the surface of the water about two hundred yards from shore; from there it returned to shore, where it made a somersault of slipknots through an "obelisk"—also natural—then rose to the peaks of two mountains in the coastal range, whence it returned to the obelisk, thereby forming a triangle. The contraption had remained intact for centuries—without needing restoration or any specialized maintenance; on the contrary, always impervious to gross and even brutal mishandling by treasure hunters (everybody, that is), predators, the merely curious, and legions of tourists.

I was just one more ... The last, as we shall see. I was quite excited to find myself face to face with it. It doesn't matter what you know about a famous object—being in its presence is altogether a different story. You must find that sensation of reality, peel back the veil of dreams—which is the substance of reality—and rise to the occasion of the moment, the Everest of the moment. Needless to say, I am not capable of such a feat, I, less than anybody. In any case, there it was ... gorgeous in its invincible, tense, and lean fragility, capturing the ancient light of navigators and adventurers. I was also able to ascertain the truth of its reputation: it was never completely silent. On stormy nights the wind made it sing, and those who heard it during a hurricane became obsessed for the rest of their lives with its cosmic howls. Sea breezes of all kinds had strummed this lyre with a single chord: memory's handmaiden, the wind. But even that afternoon, when the air was utterly still (if a bird had dropped a feather, it would have fallen to the ground in a straight line), its murmurings were thunderous. They were solemn and sharp microtones, deep within the silence.

My presence there, in front of the monument, had enormous consequences: objective, historical consequences;

not only for me but for the entire world. My discreet, un-assuming, fleeting presence, almost like that of any other tourist … Because that afternoon I solved the enigma, activated the slumbering device, and recovered the treasure from the depth of the sea.

It is not that I am a genius or exceptionally gifted, not by any means. Quite the contrary. What happened (I shall try to explain it) is that every mind is shaped by its own experiences and memories and knowledge, and what makes it unique is the grand total and extremely personal nature of the collection of all the data that have made it what it is. Each person possesses a mind with powers that are, whether great or small, always unique, powers that belong to them and to them alone. This renders them capable of carrying out a feat, whether grandiose or banal, that only they could have carried out. In this case, all others had failed because they had counted on the simple quantitative progression of intelligence and ingenuity, when what was required was an unspecified quantity, but of the appropriate quality, of both. My own intelligence is quite minimal, a fact I have ascertained at great cost to myself. It has been just barely adequate to keep me afloat in the tempestuous waters of life. Yet, its quality is unique; not because I decided it would be, but rather because that is how it must be.

This is and always has been the case in just this way with all people, at all times, everywhere. A single example taken from the world of culture (and what other world should we take it from?) might help clarify this point. An intellectual's uniqueness can be established by examining their combined readings. How many people can there be in the world who have read these two books: *The Philosophy of Life Experience* by A. Bogdanov, and *Faust* by Estanislao del Campo? Let us put aside, for the moment, any reflections these books might have provoked, how they resonated or were assimilated, all of which would necessarily be personal and nontransferable. Let us instead turn to the raw fact of the two books themselves. The concurrence of both in one reader is improbable, insofar as they belong to two distinct cultural environments and neither belongs to the canon of universal classics. Even so, it is possible that one or two dozen intellectuals across a wide swathe of time and space might have taken in this twin nourishment. As soon as we add a third book, however, let us say *La Poussière de soleil* by Raymond Roussel, that number becomes drastically reduced. If it is not "one" (that is, I), it will come very close. Perhaps it is "two," and I would have good reason to call the other "mon semblable, mon frère." One more book, a fourth, and I could be absolutely certain of my solitude. But I have not read four books; chance and curiosity have placed thousands in my hands. And besides books, and without departing from the realm of culture, there are records, paintings, movies …

All of that, as well as the texture of my days and nights since the day I was born, gave me a mental configuration different from all others. And it just so happened to be precisely the one required to solve the problem of the Macuto Line; to solve it with the greatest of ease, effortlessly, like adding two plus two. To solve it, I said, not explain it; by no means am I suggesting that the anonymous pirate who devised it was my intellectual twin. I have no twin, which is why I was able to come upon the key that unlocked the enigma, which hundreds of scholars and thousands of treasure hunters had sought in vain for four centuries—and in more recent years with access to a much broader range of resources, including deep-sea divers, sonar, computers, and teams of multidisciplinary experts. I was the only one; in a certain sense, I was the appointed one.

Though, I must warn you, not unique in the literal sense. Anybody who'd had the same experiences as I'd had (all of them, that is, because it is impossible to determine a priori which are relevant) could also have done it. And they don't even have to be literally the "same" experiences, because experiences can have equivalents.

So, I do not feel much like boasting. All the credit goes to the happenstance that placed me, precisely me, in the right place—at Las Quince Letras Hotel—one November afternoon with several hours and nothing to do (I had missed my connecting flight and had to wait until the next day). On my way there I wasn't thinking about the Macuto Line, I hadn't even remembered its existence. I was surprised to find it, a few steps away from the hotel, like a souvenir from my childhood love for books about pirates.

It just so happened, and in keeping with the rule of the law of explanations, another related enigma got solved, which was the discovery of how the rope (the "line," in question) had withstood the elements intact for such a long time. Synthetic fibers could have, but there was nothing synthetic about the Macuto Line, as exhaustive laboratory analyses had shown, analyses conducted on miniscule strands extracted with diamond-pointed tweezers: the material consisted of nothing but pine and liana fibers around a hemp core.

The solution to the main problem did not occur to me immediately. For two or three hours I was not even aware that my brain was working on it while I was taking a walk, going up to my room to write for a while, watching the sea from my window, and going out again, all in the tedium of waiting. During that interlude I had time to observe the antics of some children who were diving off some rocks into the sea some sixty feet from shore. This already constitutes part of the "short story" and, as a matter of fact, holds interest only for me. But out of such ineffable and microscopic pieces the puzzle is made. Because there is, in fact, no such thing as "in the meantime." For example, I was thinking absentmindedly about the children's game as a humble artifact construed from natural elements, one of which was the recognition of the kinetic pleasure of the plunge, the muscular contractions, the swimming-respiration ... How did they avoid those rocky ridges scattered haphazardly among the waves? How did they manage to land only inches away from a rock that would have killed them with its rigid Medusa-like caress? Habit. They probably did the same thing every afternoon. Which gave the game the weight necessary to become a legend. Those children themselves were a habit of the Macuto coast, but a legend is also a habit. And that time of day, that precise hour, twilight in the tropics, which arrives so early and at the same time is so belated, so majestic in its harmonies, that hour was part of this habit ...

Suddenly, everything fell into place. I, who only understand anything through sheer exhaustion and resignation, suddenly understood everything. I thought I'd make a note for a short novel, but why not do it for once rather than write about it? I quickly went to the platform where the Line's triangle had its vertex ... I just barely touched the bundle of knots with the tips of my fingers, turning it over without attempting to untie anything ... A humming could be heard for miles around, and the Line began to run over itself at a cosmic velocity. The mountain it was attached to seemed to shudder, surely an illusion created by the sliding of the cord, which soon spread to the section that sank into the sea. The onlookers who had been watching my actions and those who came to the windows of the nearby buildings were all looking out toward the high seas ...

And there, with a prodigious crack and a burst of foam, the treasure chest at the sunken end of the Line leapt so forcefully out of the sea that it rose about two hundred feet in the air, hung there for an instant, then shot down in a straight line, while the Line retracted, pulling back, until the treasure fell intact onto the stone platform, about three feet from where I was standing, waiting for it.

I won't go into the whole explanation here, because it would take many pages, and I have imposed upon myself a strict length limit for this text (of which this is only a prologue) out of respect for the reader's time.

What I would like to point out is that I did not limit myself to solving the enigma speculatively but also did so in practice. That is to say: after understanding what I had to do, I went and did it. And the object responded. The Line, a taut bow for centuries, finally shot its arrow, bringing to my feet the sunken treasure and instantaneously making me a wealthy man. Which was quite practical, because I have always been poor, lately more so than usual.

I had just spent a year in financial despair and, to tell the truth, had been wondering how I was going to get out of a situation that was deteriorating by the day. My literary activities, cloaked in terms of unassailable artistic purity, never rendered me much material gain. The same held true for my scientific labors, in large part due to the secrecy with which I have carried them out and about which I will speak more later. From an early age I have earned my living as a translator. With time I have perfected my professional skills and achieved a certain amount of prestige; during the last several years I enjoyed some stability though never abundance, which never bothered me as my lifestyle is quite austere. But now, the economic crisis has seriously affected the publishing business, which is paying for its previous years of euphoria. The euphoria led to oversupply, the bookstores were filled with locally produced books, and when the public needed to tighten its belt, the purchase of books was the first thing to go. Publishers, then, found themselves with huge inventories they couldn't sell, their only remaining recourse being to cut production. They cut it so much that I spent the whole year unemployed, sorrowfully spending my savings and eyeing the future with increasing anxiety. One can, thus, see how opportune this incident was for me.

Here is an additional cause for astonishment: to wonder how wealth from four hundred years ago could have retained some value, and how this value could be so enormous. Above all taking into account the speed of currency devaluations in our countries, the changes in the denomination of our currencies, and economic policies of all kinds. But I'm not going to go into that subject. On the other hand, wealth always has something inexplicable about it, more so than poverty. As of that moment, I was wealthy, and that's all there is to it. If I hadn't had to leave the next day for Mérida to fulfill a commitment I couldn't (and didn't wish to) break, I would have gone to Paris or New York to show off my newly acquired opulence.

So it was that the next morning, with my pockets full and preceded by a clamor of fame that filled all the newspapers of the world, I boarded an airplane that carried me to the beautiful Andean city where the literary conference, the subject of this story, was being held.

PART II

The Conference

IN ORDER TO MAKE myself understood, the following will need to be very clear and very detailed, even at the expense of literary elegance. Though not too profuse with details, for such an accretion can obfuscate the comprehension of the whole; moreover, and as I previously stated, I must monitor the length. In part due to the requisites of clarity (poetic fog horrifies me), and in part to my natural preference for an orderly exposition of the material, I deem it most appropriate to begin at the beginning. Not, however, at the beginning of this story but rather at the beginning of the previous one, the beginning that made it possible for there to be a story at all. Which in turn requires me to switch levels and begin with the Fable that provides the tale's logic. I will then have to do a "translation," which, if carried out in full, would take more pages than I have assigned as the maximum number for this book; thus I will "translate" only when necessary; all other fragments of the Fable will remain in the original language; and though I am aware that this might affect its credibility, I believe it to be the preferred solution. By way of supplemental warning, I would like to add that the Fable in question takes its logic from a prior Fable, on yet another level of discourse; similarly on the other end, the story provides the immanent logic to another story, thus ad infinitum. And (in conclusion) I have filled these plots with contents that have between them a relationship of only approximate equivalencies, not meanings.

So, once upon a time … an Argentinean scientist conducted experiments in the cloning of cells, organs, and limbs, and achieved the ability to reproduce, at will, whole individuals in indefinite quantities. First, he worked with insects, then higher animals, and finally human beings. His success did not vary, though as he approached human beings the nature of the clones subtly changed; they became non-similar clones. He overcame his disappointment with this variation by telling himself that in the final analysis the perception of similarity is quite subjective and always questionable. He had no doubt, however, that his clones were genuine, legions of Ones whose numbers he could multiply as often as he wished.

At this point he reached an impasse and found himself unable to proceed toward his final goal, which was nothing less than world domination. In this respect he was the typical Mad Scientist of the comic books. He was incapable of setting a more modest goal for himself; at his level, it simply wouldn't have been worth his while. He then discovered that to achieve this final goal, his armies of clones (virtual, in the meantime, because for practical reasons he had created only a few samples) were utterly useless.

In a certain sense he had become a prisoner of his own success, according to the classic depiction of the Mad Scientist, who, in the course of the adventure itself, in the politics of the action, always ends up defeated, no matter how great his previous achievements in the field of science have been. Fortunately for him, he was not truly mad—his thirst for power had not blinded him; around the edges he retained enough lucidity to change the direction of his experiments. This was possible due to the material conditions under which he carried them out: the precarious conditions of a do-it-yourself amateur, making do with cardboard boxes and bottles, with recycled toys and bargain basement made-in-China retorts. He had set up his laboratory in the tiny servant's room in his old apartment; as he had no morgue, he let his human clones roam the streets of the neighborhood. Poverty, which had caused him so much frustration, revealed its positive aspect when he saw that he could only achieve his goals by radically transforming his methods, something he could do without any adverse effect on his investments or installations, which either didn't exist or were worth nothing at all.

The problem, and the solution, were the following: he could create a human being from a single cell, a being that was identical in body and soul to the specimen from which the cell was taken. One or many, as many as he wished. Up to this point, everything was okay. The only difficulty, paradoxical if you wish, is that these creatures had to be at his mercy. He could not be at their mercy. They could obey him, but he couldn't obey them; he saw no reason to do so: they were beings with no prestige, no ideas, no originality. This circumstance thwarted all further action, for he still had to carry the burden of the initiative. And what could he do, even as the general in charge of countless legions, to achieve his ultimate goal of world domination? Declare war? Launch an assault against those in power? It would be his to lose. He didn't even have weapons, nor did he know how to acquire them; weapons could not be reproduced through cloning; cloning worked only on living organic material; thus, life was the only element he could count on. And the mere multiplication of life cannot be considered a weapon, at least not under his conditions, through cloning. The miracle of the spontaneous creation of an additional nervous system was cancelled out by stripping it, from the outset, of the ability to give orders, and with that, to create.

It was on this point that our Mad Scientist most differed from the stereotype of the Mad Scientist, who would typically dig in his heels with self-destructive resolve in order to maintain the central role of his own intellect. Ours reached the conclusion that he could only manage to take a "leap forward" from his current stage if he found a way to get out from the middle, if his intellect could be placed at the service of another intellect, his power at the service of another greater power ... if his will deteriorated within a system of external gravitations. Therein lay his unparalleled originality (as far as Mad Scientists go): in recognizing that "another" idea is always more efficient than "an" idea, by the mere virtue of being an-other. And an idea does not get enriched through expansion or multiplication (clones) but rather by passing through another brain.

So, what to do? The obvious solution was to clone a superior man ... Though choosing which one was not a simple matter. Superiority is a relative condition and eminently subject to disagreement. Above all, it is not easy to decide from one's own point of view, which is the only point of view at one's disposition. And the adoption of objective criteria can be deceptive; be that as it may, he had no choice but to adopt some kind of objective criteria, which he would then need to refine. In the first instance, he had to disregard statistical appearances, such as would predominate in a survey, which would skew the sample toward those at the top of the visible pyramid of power: heads of state, business magnates, generals ... No. Just thinking about this put a smile on his lips, the same smile he could well imagine appearing on the lips of those who wielded true power upon hearing those words. Because life experience had taught him that, say what you will, real power—which makes one smile with disdain at apparent power—resided in a different kind of person whose central and defining acquisition was high culture: Philosophy, History, Literature, the Classics. The self-proclaimed stand-ins from popular culture and advanced technology, and those who had accumulated enormous fortunes through financial manipulation, were ineffectual shams. In fact, high culture's disguise as something old fashioned and out-of-date was the perfect strategy to disorient the unsuspecting masses. This is why high culture continued to be the almost exclusive privilege of the upper classes. But the Mad Scientist wasn't even thinking of cloning a member of that class. Precisely because they were so fully guaranteed the exercise of definitive and ultimate power, and because this guarantee lasted throughout all successive generations, they didn't suit his purposes. Then he thought of resorting to a great criminal, but this was a romantic notion, compelling only for its Nietzschean resonance, and at its core, absurd.

Finally, he decided on what was simplest and most effective: a Celebrity. A recognized and celebrated Genius. To clone a genius! This was the decisive step. This would set him firmly on the road to world domination (because, among other reasons, he'd already covered half of it). He felt the excitement of a momentous moment. Beyond this decision, he had no need to make plans or harbor hopes, for everything would be placed, "invested," in the Great Man, who would take charge because he was superior. As for the scientist, he would remain free from all responsibility—other than his role as the bootlicker, the heinous clown—and his own incompetence, his poverty and his blunders, would no longer matter; on the contrary, they would become his trump cards.

He chose his genius carefully, or better said, he didn't need to choose him because fate placed him in his path, within reach: the most unassailable and undisputed genius there could ever be; his level of respectability touched on the transcendent. This was his natural target, and he set to work without further delay.

To say that he had him "within reach" is an exaggeration; in our celebrity culture, celebrities live isolated behind impregnable walls of privacy and move around inside invisible fortresses nobody can breach. But the same opportunity that had called him to his attention also brought him more or less close by ... He didn't need to be too close. All he needed was one cell from his body, any cell, for each one contains the information necessary to clone the entire individual. Unwilling to trust fate to afford him the opportunity to obtain a hair or a nail trimming or a flake of skin, he employed one of his most trusted creatures, a small wasp reduced to the size of a period and loaded from birth with the identifying data of the aforementioned Genius; he sent her on her secret mission at noon under conditions of certain proximity (the wasp has a very short flight range). He trusted her blindly for he knew her to be at the mercy of the infallible force of instinct, of never-erring Nature. And she did not disappoint him: ten minutes later she returned, carrying the cell on her feet ... He immediately placed it on the slide of his pocket microscope and became ecstatic. The strength of his strategy was confirmed: it was a gorgeous cell, deep, filled with languages, iridescent, a limpid blue with transparent highlights. He'd never seen such a cell, it almost didn't seem human. He placed it in the portable cloning machine he had brought with him, called a taxi, told the driver to take him to the highest plateau in the vicinity, continued from there on foot for a few hours, and when he had reached windswept heights where he was gasping for breath, he looked around for a remote spot to leave the machine. Incubation on a mountain peak was not a poetic detail: the specific conditions of pressure and temperature at these altitudes were what the process required: to reproduce them artificially he would need to be in his modest laboratory, from which he was separated by thousands of miles, and he feared the cell would not survive the rigors of the journey, or would lose its vitality. He left it there and climbed down. Now all he could do was wait ...

Here I must attempt a first and partial translation. The "Mad Scientist" is, of course, me. The identification of the Genius may end up being more problematic, but it's not worth wasting time with conjectures: it is Carlos Fuentes. If I agreed to go to that conference in Mérida it was only after I had confirmation that he would attend; I needed to get close enough so that my cloned wasp could take a cell from him. It was a unique opportunity to gain access to him for my scientific manipulations. They served him to me on a platter, and I didn't even have to spend money on an airplane ticket, which I wouldn't have been able to afford, given how bad things had been lately. Or how they had been before the Macuto Line episode. I had had a terrible year, without work, a result of the seriousness of the economic crisis, which especially affected publishing. In spite of this, I had not interrupted my experiments, because at the level on which I was working, I didn't need money. In addition to suiting to a tee the pursuit of my secret goals, this invitation to the conference gave me the opportunity to spend a week in the tropics and take a vacation; rest, recuperate, and refresh myself after a year of constant worries.

Upon my return to the hotel, the excitement of the past few hours reached its anticlimax. The first part of the operation, the most demanding part for me, was over: I had obtained a cell from Carlos Fuentes, I had placed it inside the cloning machine, and I had left the machine to operate under optimum conditions. If you add to this the fact that the previous day I had solved the secular enigma of the Macuto Line, I could feel momentarily satisfied and think about other things. I had a few days to do just that. Cloning a living being is not like blowing glass. It happens on its own, but it takes time. Even though the process is prodigiously accelerated, it requires almost a week, according to the human calendar, for it must reconstruct on a small scale the entire geology of the evolution of life.

All I could do was wait. In the meantime, I had to figure out how to spend my time. As I had no intention of attending the tedious sessions of the conference, I bought a bathing suit and, beginning the following day, I spent mornings and afternoons at the swimming pool.

II

At the swimming pool, I focused all my efforts on one goal: to reduce my mental hyperactivity. To let myself be, naked under the sun. To create internal silence. I have pursued this goal through all of life's twists and turns, almost like an idée fixe. This is the small and alarming idea that stands out in the midst of all other ideas and raises the volume of psychic noise, which is already quite considerable. Hyperactivity has become my brain's normal way of being. It's always been like that, to tell the truth, at least since my adolescence, and I've learned about the more normal way most other people are—hesitant and half-empty—through reading, observation, deduction, and conjecture. And because, on a few occasions, for a few seconds, I have had that experience. My readings in Eastern psychic techniques, and even those stupid articles about "meditation" that often appear in women's magazines, have taught me that there is one further step: an empty mind, the complete or almost complete lack of electrical activity in the cerebral cortex, a blackout, rest. And if at one time, with my characteristic ambitiousness,

I, too, wished to achieve that, and practiced all the recommended exercises with innocent trust, I finally grew convinced that I was wasting my time. It wasn't for me. First, I would have to descend from my peaks of frenzy, take hold of the reins, and mollify the runaway beast of my thoughts, force it to slow to a normal pace; only then would I have a chance to glimpse those Eastern worlds of spiritual serenity.

I have often asked myself how I got into this situation, what happened during my formative years that increased the speed of my mental flow so excessively and made it stick there. I have also asked myself (what haven't I asked myself?) what the exact measure of that speed is, for the very concept of "mental hyperactivity" is approximate and must contain gradations.

To the first question, regarding the history of my malady, I have responded for better or for worse with a small and private "creation myth," whose modulations have been all the novels I have written. I would be hard put to spell this out in the abstract because the myths' variations are not specific "examples" of a general form, in the same way that specific thoughts that are always flashing through my head like lightning are not case studies or examples of a type of thought.

That myth of the ideal myriads, that little drama without characters or plot, would be shaped like a valve. Or, in less technical terms, it would have the characteristic Baudelaire called "irreversibility." A formulated thought does not pass back through the same Caudine forks of its birth, does not return to the nothingness from which it came. Which explains not only the fierce overcrowding but also a quite visible feature of my personality: my bewilderment, my imprudence, my frivolity. The withdrawal of an idea to the conditions of its production is the necessary condition for its seriousness.

In my case, nothing returns, everything races forward, savagely being pushed from behind by what keeps coming through that accursed valve. This image, brought to its peak of maturation in my vertiginous reflections, revealed to me the path to the solution, which I forcefully put into practice whenever I have time and feel like it. The solution is none other than the greatly overused (by me) "escape forward." Since turning back is off limits: Forward! To the bitter end! Running, flying, gliding, using up all the possibilities, the conquest of tranquility through the din of the battlefield. The vehicle is language. What else? Because the valve is language. Therein lay the root of the problem. Which doesn't mean that once in a while, such as during those sessions at the pool, I didn't attempt a more conventional method, by relaxing, by trying to forget everything, by taking a short vacation.

But I have no illusions: there's something phony about this effort because I don't believe I'll ever renounce my old and beloved cerebral hyperactivity, which, in the end, is what I am. Despite all our plans to change, we never voluntarily do so at the core, in our essence, which is usually where we find the knot of our worst defects. I could change it—and I surely would have already—if it were a visible defect, like a limp or acne; but it isn't. The rest of the world has no inkling of the mental whirlwinds swirling under my impassive facade, except, perhaps, through the amplification of that impassivity, or through certain digressions I engage in and abandon without warning. Or perhaps, for a superhuman literary critic, through my relationship with language. My cerebral hyperactivity makes itself manifest inside me (and language is my bridge to the exterior) with rhetorical or quasi-rhetorical mechanisms. These then get distorted in a very peculiar fashion. Take metaphor, for example: everything is a metaphor in the hyperkinetic microscope of my psyche, everything is instead of something else...But you cannot extract yourself unscathed from the whole: the whole creates a system of pressures that distorts the metaphors, moving their parts around between metaphors, thereby establishing a continuum.

"Rising above" this situation requires an enormous effort of art-science in the face of which I have not, of course, recoiled. But I engage in this effort on my own terms. Heisenberg's principle also comes into play here: observation modifies the object of observation and increases its velocity. Under my interior magnifying glass, or inside it, each thought takes on the figure of a clone in its rhetorical anamorphosis: an overdetermined identity.

Which reminds me of the answer to the question I left hanging: how to measure the velocity of my thoughts.

I am trying a method of my own invention: I shoot a perfectly empty thought through all the others, and because it has no content of its own, it reveals the furtive outlines—which are stable in the empty one—of the contents of the others. That retrograde cloned mini-man, the Speedometer, is my companion on solitary walks and the only one who knows all my secrets.

III

Just as I am total thought, I am total body. This is not a contradiction. All the totals get superimposed upon each other ... The concept of "totals" is fairly slippery; only a subject in motion can confront it, and the moment that subject is able to enunciate it, it becomes a truth. It was the truth within the restricted Universe of those days of rest I allowed myself under the tropical sun in the swimming pool of a luxury hotel on the outskirts of the city while my operation was underway. I regretted it would last for only the few days of a single week; the pleasure of such delicious passivity could only make me wish that life in its totalness was like that, the total world, the total of totals. It was natural for me to slip into totals. My body accepted it, swelled up with it, radiated it. To top it off, the weather was perfect. Few people went to the pool: several youngsters, male and female, some children with their mothers, one or another loner like me ... Some mornings nobody was there. The caretaker swam melancholically, lap after lap, dozed in his chair, and amused himself trying to catch drowned mosquitoes floating just under the surface of the water using a net with a very fine mesh. The water was as clear as well-washed crystal: you could have read a newspaper floating on the bottom. My hosts at the conference told me it was logical so few people went … In fact, they couldn't believe it when I told them I was not the only one there. Who would ever think, they exclaimed, of going swimming in the middle of winter? It's true, it was winter, but being so close to the equator, it made no difference to me; as far as I was concerned it was still summer, and it continued to be a totality of summer, and life.

One curious thing I noticed and wish to make note of in this report is that all of us who went to the pool those few days, without knowing each other or having planned anything at all among us, were perfect specimens of the human race. What I mean is, we all looked human, with all our members and corresponding muscles and nerves in their proper places and proportions. Physical perfection in the human is rare by definition, for the slightest defect nullifies it. If you look at people in the street, scarcely one in a hundred passes the test. All the rest are monsters. But, to my languid surprise, those of us who came to the pool (different ones every day, except me) constituted a gathering of that one percent. I wonder if it isn't always like that, in every unplanned encounter. Be that as it may, what with the swimmers wearing only bathing suits, their bodies exposed to the sun, there was no room for denial. The spectacle soothed my eyes and my mind. I didn't look for defects, because there were none; in a certain sense, there couldn't be any. Deviations from the physical canon produce monsters; all kinds of monsters, even imperceptible ones. One toe slightly wider or longer than it should be is enough to create some sort of monster. One cell, a spelling mistake within a cell … For some reason, monsters manage to escape from the net that brings humans to the surface. They remain floating like Cartesian devils in the half-light of unreality. I know a lot about such things because this is the branch of science I practice.

Perfections, on the contrary, are all different: perfection in itself is the perfection or full expression of difference. This is why cultivating perfection means collaborating with what a young disciple once defined as the task we should dedicate our lives to: giving birth to the individual.

My daydreams left me paralyzed. For hours I would lie cataleptic in my lounge chair. The art of perfecting the body could only be practiced during an eternal summer, or an eternal day, or an endless life … But, like the seasons in the tropics, like this anachronistic autumnal summer, such eternities must be silhouetted against an alien psyche, and be invisible to all.

Wasn't this method more practical than cloning? Was there anything stopping me from adopting it? Now that I was rich, thanks to the Macuto Line (it had happened so recently I still wasn't used to the idea), I could settle in under that sky and live naked under the sun without worrying about anything. I wouldn't even have to change my field. Literature, cloning … transformations … I have become convinced of what I consider to be the basic premise of everything I will ever do in my life: all transformations occur *without the least expenditure of energy*. This is fundamental. If effort were required, even the most minimal amount—and given that in a transformation the point of departure and arrival are identical, i.e. the "transformed"—energy

César Aira

would be left over and would, in turn, inflate one end or the other of the universe, creating a bulge and returning us to the realm of the monstrous.

But no. I was roused from these fantasies when I remembered the work at hand. I dove into the water one last time, swam for a while in the now-deserted pool, then walked around the edge, letting the setting sun and the gentle breeze from the highlands dry me off. All around me I could see the mountains and their snow-covered peaks. Up there, in some inaccessible spot, the cloning machine, the hidden heart of the heights, was carrying out its secret task.

My shadow stretched out in front of me, a human shadow, but also alien, irreconcilable. I stretched out my arms, and the arms of the shadow did the same; I lifted a leg, bent at the waist, turned my head, and the shadow imitated me. Would it do the same if I stretched out the fingers on one of my hands? I tried it. I abandoned myself to a dance of recognition ... The other bathers watched me out of the corners of their eyes, discreetly ... When you are traveling the thought that nobody knows you gives you a certain feeling of impunity. That wasn't the case with me. The breeze carried snippets of their conversations, and I realized they were talking about me: "famous writer ... Macuto Line ... he was in the newspapers ..."

Impunity: it's always impunity that gets you dancing. What did I care about being ridiculous? I was on my way to earning a superior kind of impunity, and nobody knew it.

IV

The only interruption to this rash of days of repose and swimming was on Wednesday night, when I felt obliged to perform a very private ceremony. That afternoon, the wasp had died.

Two days earlier, I returned her to the cage I had carried her in from Buenos Aires after she had brought me a cell from Carlos Fuentes. When I decided to bring her, I knew that for her it would be a one-way trip. Those insects have very short lives, and by the time she was five days old, hers, in fact, had already been a long one. Once she had completed her mission, I didn't need her anymore and could have destroyed her, as well as her little cage, and thereby left no trace of my activities. Traveling with her brought with it a touch of risk, so I kept her hidden. Despite there being no law regarding the international transport of cloned materials, the custom agents' sensitivities to the transport of drugs, genetic mutations, and bacterial weapons could have created problems. I had no choice but to bring her, so I took the chance. Luckily nothing happened.

Nor did I want anybody at the hotel to know of her existence: my scientific activities are secret; giving explanations would have put me on the spot, especially if it became known that I was experimenting with a renowned Mexican author. All things considered, disposing of the wasp the moment I no longer needed her would have been the most prudent thing to do; and I needn't have felt any scruples for she would anyway have soon died a natural death. But my loyalty to my little creature won the day. I preferred to wait for her to perish on her own, complete her own life cycle, as if Nature were mediating between her and me according to Her own sacrosanct laws.

Even though I didn't trust the hotel maids, with their curiosity and brutality, I left her in the room. I could have carried her in my pocket wherever I went, but I trusted the maids more than my own absentmindedness: I'm always losing things, or leaving them somewhere, anywhere. So, I left her in the room for whole days at a time during my interminable sessions at the pool. Under lock and key, of course. Fortunately, I had no occasion for regret. Upon returning to my room, I'd take her out and place the little cage on my bedside table while I read lying down or napped. In addition to my sense of loyalty, there must have been an element of sentimentality or loneliness: after all, she was company, a reminder of my life at home and in my laboratory, a minuscule Argentinean spark.

To speak of "wasp" or "insect" as I have is an abusive oversimplification; they are words I use, as I do repeatedly in this book, only to make myself understood. To create my "wasp," I used wasp DNA, that's true, because I needed certain wasp traits, but I used them only as a "mannequin" (I resort to specialized jargon) for other traits my mission required and that I extracted from my gene catalogue. If I chose the wasp mannequin over that of, say, the dragonfly or the bee, it was because of its greater ability to bond with foreign genes. But the resulting critter had little in common with a wasp: for starters, it was the size of a speck of dust. Under the microscope, she looked more like a golden sea horse with strong mothlike wings shaped like fans, and something between a rhinoceros horn and a crab claw—though articulated—sprouted from her head: this was the cell punch. All of these—and more—exist in zoology. She was a prototype, a unique specimen, a nice little monster that would never be repeated.

As I was saying, I found her dead upon my return from the pool on Wednesday afternoon. Her life had been consummated in less than one week: it began in Argentina and ended in Venezuela, several thousand miles to the north. I contemplated her briefly and felt sad without knowing why. Her cadaver, which had become translucent and acquired a touch of an amber hue, was nothing more than a spot on the floor of her little house that nobody else would ever inhabit because I had built it for her. When earlier I spoke of "cage," I did so, once again, to simplify things; it was, in fact, a cubicle the size of a thimble made of cellophane, which on a whim I fashioned into the shape of a Swiss chalet, with a pressurized chamber made of lamprey eel genes. I'm such a perfectionist that if there were a gene for furnishings, I would have made her a beautiful trousseau.

Night came. I went down to eat, then killed some time in the bar until eleven o'clock. Uncustomarily, I drank a cup of coffee. I never do so at that time of day, because then I cannot sleep, and I am terrified of insomnia. But that night I would stay up, because I had already devised a plan of action. Moreover, considering that overdetermination I know so well, how it gets set in motion and proliferates as soon as an action begins, I would need one of the coffee implements: the spoon, which I stole. It was a beautiful silver spoon with a clown engraved on the handle.

A short while later, after telling my bar companions that I was going to sleep, I left the hotel. The city was deserted. I went in the opposite direction from downtown; the road climbed steeply until it reached the highway that encircles the city; once past that, I found myself in open country in the foothills of the mountains. I continued walking for several hundred yards, until I could no longer hear the automobiles. The only light was the light of the stars, but they were so bright, so captivating, so close, that I could see everything, far and near: the blunt masses of the rocks, the deep recesses of the valley, the river flowing under the bridges.

The precise spot didn't matter, and the one I was in was as good as any other, so I reached my hand into my pocket and took out the tiny corpse. At that moment I observed some movement among the dark masses around my feet, which I had assumed were rocks. I looked more carefully and saw that they were all moving with the slowness and regularity of zombies. They were turkey vultures, those black buzzards who spent their days hovering over the valley. Seeing them perched like that for the first time, I thought they looked like small, gloomy hunchbacked chickens. It appears I had happened upon one of their mountainside bedrooms. The walking around I was witnessing may have been due to having woken them up with my intrusion, or perhaps they really were zombies. They seemed the perfect funeral cortege for my wasp's burial. I set to work.

With my spoon I dug a round hole about two inches wide and almost eight deep, at the bottom of which I carved out a nearly circular burial chamber; there I placed the tiny cellophane Swiss chalet with its eternal resident. I sealed the entrance with a coin and filled the vertical tunnel with dirt that I pressed down with my thumb. I placed a triangular-shaped pebble on top for a gravestone.

I stood up and dedicated a final thought to my wasp. Goodbye little friend! Goodbye...! We would never see each other again, but I would never forget her ... I would never be able to forget her, even if I wanted to. Because nothing could replace her. Excitement mixed with melancholy. The Mad Scientist (and I, myself, on another level of this story's meaning) could boast about the unprecedented luxury of having made the entire evolutionary process serve a unique and determined—as well as subsidiary—purpose, almost like going to buy a newspaper ... I needed somebody to get me a cell belonging to

Carlos Fuentes, and for that reason, and no other, I created a being within which converged millions of years and many more millions of fine points of selection, adaptation, and evolution ... to carry out a unique service and thereby complete its purpose; a throw-away creature, as if the miracle that is man had been created one afternoon just so he could walk over to the door to look outside and see if it were raining, and once this task had been accomplished, he would be annihilated. Needless to say, the cloning procedure reduced such excessive periods of natural labor to a few days, though they remained, essentially, the same.

V

The moment has come, I believe, to do another "translation" of the story I am telling in order to make clear my true intentions. My Great Work is secret, clandestine, and encompasses my life in its entirety, even its most insignificant folds and those that seem the most banal. Until now I have concealed my purpose under the accommodating guise of literature. Because I am a writer, this causes no particular concern.

Marginally, this pretense has afforded me certain mundane pleasures, and an acceptable modus vivendi. But my goal—which in my quest for transparency has become my best kept secret—is typical of the comic-book Mad Scientist: to extend my dominion over the entire world.

I am aware that we have here a metaphorical alibi; "dominion" and "world" are words, and the sentence containing them lends itself to intellectual, philosophical, and paradoxical interpretations ... I refuse to fall into that trap. The dominion I'm talking about wants to be extended across reality, the "world" is none other than the objective, shared world ... The only paradox, if there is one, is that language has shaped our expectations so extensively that real reality has become the most detached and incomprehensible one of all.

The opening of the doors of reality is the infinite pro-legomenon to my Great Work. And I have already made reference to one of these "doors" (an inoffensive meta-phor): perfection. From there to the pool. My brain: the battlefield.

After a certain age, doubt threatens the perfection of the body. Assessing ourselves objectively is difficult be-cause we continue to think of ourselves as adolescent, and others always have a reason to lie. Perfection becomes a longing, sometimes all-consuming. We would do any-thing to achieve it, we really would: any diet, any exercise. We would not shrink from any effort. But we don't know what that "anything" is and have no way of finding out. If we ask ten people, we get ten different answers. And thus we squander the most genuine of longings. We would do whatever was necessary … if we knew what that was. But we don't.

As a result, perfection has to find its own way. We can't find perfection. The miracle is that it happens at all. Life is generous that way, it always is.

If the preceding text were a riddle, I would not need to provide the answer, not even written upside down at the foot of this page, because any reader could have guessed it right away: love. Love, the portentous coincidence, the surprise, the flower of this world.

Until now, I have been drawing a portrait of a character who represents me in more or less fair and realistic—even if partial—terms. Until now, he could have been taken for a cold, clear-headed scientist writing a well-reasoned memoir in which even emotions take on an icy edge ... To complete the portrait, though, we would need to paint in a background of passion, so alive and excessive that it makes the rest tremble.

It would be counterproductive to go into too many details, so I won't. I know myself and I know that the triumph of my false modesty when I sit down to write would translate into such absurd fairy tales that I don't know where it would end up. I'll say only what's most basic; better: I'll sketch it out.

Years ago, in this same city, at this same pool, I met a woman and fell in love with her. I couldn't and didn't want to commit myself, so I returned to Buenos Aires and my life there, but I couldn't forget Amelina. I should add that we did not remain in touch, not even epistolary touch, because when I left I forgot to write down her address—a meaningful lapse. To tell the truth, I didn't feel I had the right to love her. She was young enough to be my daughter, she studied literature, and she was innocent in a way that is difficult to describe. As for me, I was married, with children, dedicated to my secret scientific endeavors that forced me into Machiavellian contortions ... What kind of future could we have? The opportunity passed, and by the same token, didn't pass. Amelina's love continued to reside within me and remained a constant source of inspiration. Now, upon my return, I thought of her ... But Amelina didn't appear. She was still living in the city, as

I discovered by accident, and she must have read in the newspapers of my presence, but she kept her distance. She was avoiding me. I understood and accepted. Moreover, I wasn't even sure I'd recognize her if I saw her again. A lot of time had passed, she'd probably gotten married …

It was an old story, older than she was in reality. When I met Amelina, it was love at first sight, overwhelming, a whirlwind … This was because the current carried me way back, back to a time when I, too, had loved. By the time I met Amelina, I was already a grown man, I had lost almost all hope, I felt defeated, I believed nothing could bring back my lost youth. And nothing did, obviously. But when I saw Amelina, I miraculously recognized in her features, her voice, her eyes, a woman who had been my great passion when I was twenty. I had loved the beautiful Florencia to despair (ours was an impossible love) with all the madness of adolescence, and I never stopped loving her. It wasn't meant to be, we took different paths, she got married, I did too, we lived in the same neighborhood, sometimes I saw her walk by with her children as they were growing up … Twenty years passed, thirty … She gained weight, that delicate and shy girl I had adored turned into a mature woman full of middle-class respectability … She must be a grandmother by now. How incredible! How life flies by! For the heart, time doesn't pass.

Florencia had been reborn, in all the splendor of her youth, in the sweet Amelina, whom I had had to cross a continent to find. I sensed their resemblance in the smallest of details, in the most intimate folds of their smiles, or of their dreams. The coincidence spanned a lifetime, and in the magical wonder it brought me, I found the justification for my work: during the years following my encounter with Amelina, my Great Work took off, embarked on a definitive direction, and I began to see the fruits of my labor. She was my Muse.

All well and good. On Thursday afternoon, I was dozing in my lounge chair by the pool when suddenly something made me lift my head and look around. At first it didn't seem like anything very special was going on: the few bathers who were often there at that time of day were quiet, some conversed in low voices, several children were playing in the water. In the sky: the omnipresent turkey vultures. Nevertheless, I could feel it: something was stirring in that uneventful calm … I knew I was in a prophetic state, as if possessed. What was about to happen was already happening. I leapt up, light and heavy at once, a statue made of floating metal, and walked over to the edge of the deck. On the other side of the pool, right in front of me, rose a living statue. I have never felt so naked. It was Amelina, larger than life (or smaller?), in subtle colors that seemed to have been gleaned from the noontime shadows. She looked at me. I understood that I was hallucinating because I saw her as she had been so many years before, almost a child who was discovering me with all the surprise of a romantic adventure. But she was real, or there was something real about her. There's always something real in what happens, no avoiding that. But her skin tone was too strange, as was the light that outlined her figure, which seemed set apart from the atmospheric light. This was due, I noticed with amazement, to the fact that her figure projected no shadow onto the ground. Instantly, in a very rapid psychic sequence, I realized that I also had no shadow and that the sun had disappeared from the sky, which I confirmed when I raised my eyes. The perfectly blue sky of four o'clock in the afternoon, without a single cloud ... had no sun. It had evaporated.

I looked again at Amelina. Monumental transparent shapes in continual metamorphosis were rising from the water in the pool that separated us. I thought it was another Macuto Line, the one of dreams, the private ...

Suddenly, Amelina disappeared, the shapes melded into a horizontal wave, and the sun was once again shining in the sky. My shadow stretched out in front of me once again ... My shadow, in every swimming pool in the Andes.

I couldn't help glancing up at the mountains in the vicinity of where I had left the cloning machine. That gesture had the virtue of returning me to reality. At least I could be sure that what was happening there was not a dream. No matter what strange paths my thoughts might take, the process would continue, independently of me, though subsequently I would take charge of it. That, however, would be a kind of epilogue; in itself, the Great Work consisted principally of me abstaining from all and every intervention, of achieving a parallel trajectory of absolute integrity.

VI

There is another coincidence on another level: that be-tween the velocity of thought and thought itself. This is the same as saying that the Great Work—the creation of the individual—is exactly what is accomplished during a life span at that constant velocity. In a certain sense, veloc-ity is the Great Work; confusion arises about the method. Thus, my Great Work, my secret labor, is highly personal, nontransferable, nobody but I could carry it out, because it consists of the innumerable psychic and physical in-stants whose sequence confirms my velocity. The veloc-ity at which I unfold through time. By becoming an indi-vidual, my work allows me to love and be loved.

The aforesaid occurred to me while I was considering, with amazement, the quantity of things that were hap-pening to me while nothing was happening. I noticed this as my pen was moving: there were thousands of tiny inci-dents, all full of meaning. I've had to pick and choose care-fully, otherwise the list would be endless. But it's normal for more things to happen when you're traveling than dur-ing the normal course of habitual life. Not only because they actually happen because one is on the move and

actively going out looking for things, but because our per-
ceptions awaken when we leave our habits behind, we see
more and hear more, we even dream more. For someone
who travels as little as I do, for someone who leads such a
routine life, a trip can make an enormous difference; it is
the objective equivalent of cerebral hyperactivity.

I am selecting, somewhat haphazardly, the facts I use to
carry forward this story of the days I spent waiting while
the cloning process was taking place at the top of the
mountain, focusing exclusively on the translation possibilities. I should mention that the literary conference I
had been invited to attend was taking place concurrently,
but I was so detached from it I would not have been able
to name even one of the subjects of its sessions and panel
discussions. In one, however, I was a participant, and although this participation, fortunately, was passive and
indirect, I had no choice but to know about it. It was a
marginal activity, attendance optional, held outside the
framework of the official sessions; it consisted of the stag-
ing of one of my plays by the University Theater Group
of the Humanities Department. They had, apparently, already staged other plays of mine, and this time they had
chosen one called *In the Court of Adam and Eve*. It was not
the one I would have chosen, but I did not object when
I saw it on the program they sent me months earlier. As
soon as I arrived they asked me to attend the final rehears-
als, approve the costumes and sets, meet the actors ... I po-
litely declined. I wished to be merely another member of
the audience. That last statement was made out of a sense

of obligation, for I didn't care whether I saw it or not, and if it had been up to me, I wouldn't have gone; but it turned out to be true. As far as their request that I speak to the cast about my motivation for writing it, firmer reasons accompanied my refusal. The first one, I considered it inadvisable to explain; the others had to do with the amount of time that had passed since I'd written it, and how totally I had forgotten it. We left it at that, and though they were probably disappointed, they did not seem offended.

Nevertheless, I did intervene on one point. The play would be performed for the general public in a newly built theater, but only those attending the conference would see the preview, and that performance could be held in a different venue, possibly in the open air, thereby taking full advantage of the climate. They asked my opinion, and in this case I felt I did have something to say. They expected me to come up with something unexpected and extravagant, so I chose the airport, which is right downtown because Mérida takes up the entire small valley in which it is situated. They liked that idea, got authorization, and made all the arrangements.

The play dates back to my Darwinian period, but it foreshadows my subsequent work with clones. Within the entire body of my work, it is an exception: I have an aversion to what is now called "intertextuality," and I never make literary allusions in my novels or plays. I force myself to invent everything; when the only choice is to recycle something that already exists, I prefer to take recourse in reality. But I allowed myself this exception because Genesis is a special case, even if only for its title. If inventiveness, or the transmutation of reality, is part of a broader mechanism of literary genetics, Genesis could well be considered the master plan, at least among us Westerners.

Saying that this short play foreshadowed my subsequent scientific work is, to tell the truth, an understatement. The mere idea of Adam and Eve's existence, of humanity (the species) retroactively reduced to a single couple, gives rise to genetics. I would even say that it is as far as the imagination can go in this field. Genetics is the genesis of diversity. But if diversity has nobody on whom to spread itself out, it turns on itself, gets tangled up in its own general particularity, and therein the imagination is born.

I remember how one critic, at the play's debut many years ago, called it "a beautiful love story." In retrospect, I have found in that play the key to my difficulty in speaking about love other than through complex translations of perspectives. The coincidence of Adam with Eve in a world where it was unnecessary to seek each other out through the exhaustive labyrinths of the real is one theory of love. The passage from Adam to Eve under the guise of the fable of the rib was simply cloning. Once both characters were in the scene, cloning collapsed, decisively. The level of the fable guaranteed it would belong to an inaccessible past, a past that could only be captured through the imagination or through fiction. I believe that this myth is what turned the past into a mental construct; if not for its intercession, today we would perhaps be dealing with the past as simply one more reality, like any other object of perception.

As it turned out, sex remained the only path to repro-
duction. Sex, and the concomitant maneuverings of love.
The scenes with Adam and Eve occurred in such close
proximity to cloning—of which they had been involun-
tary protagonists—that the fable contaminated their con-
jugal passion. To the same degree I had made *sexuation* a
personal taboo, I approached them with the trembling of
monstrous familiarity.

I now begin to remember in greater detail the period
of my life when I wrote that piece. I understand why I
wanted to obscure it behind a cloud of voluntary obliv-
ion, because it was a dark moment in my life, perhaps the
worst, the most disturbed. My marriage had undergone
some very demanding trials, I was obsessed with divorce,
which, at the same time, seemed the only solution and
caused me unendurable fear. I began to drink too much,
and as my constitution is averse to alcohol, I began to de-
velop rather grotesque symptoms; the worst was a con-
traction of my left leg, which began to behave as if it were
eight inches shorter than my right; as far as I know, my
two legs are exactly the same length, but for months I was
going around with quite a conspicuous limp. This, on top
of everything else, led me to take drugs (the only time in
my life I've ever done so). I became addicted to proxidine
and so severely abused it that I would have died of an over-
dose if I had not finally found a way out.

Part of my recovery, in any case the testament to it, was
the writing of this play. Which explains my use of a pre-
existent myth. This may seem like excessive justification

for my falling into a literary trap I deplore, but so it goes, that's the way the cookie crumbles. Deep down, the marriage of Adam and Eve was the myth of absolute contingency: sex preceded and made possible by cloning; proxidine produced the same effect in my cells five times a day. But once everything reverted to literature, my recovery was complete.

In another confluent episode, which memory now holds out to me in a gesture that seems to say, "There's more where that comes from," I had a kind of fleeting hallucination, though in the midst of so many perceptual changes brought about by my drug use, I didn't pay much attention to it. Every time I closed my eyes I would see two men hurling themselves against each other, like two swordsmen, but without swords; I would see them in profile, sharply outlined, both dressed in black. The scene had very little depth, almost like an animated painting, but it was infused with a terrible level of violence.

I would immediately open my eyes, and the scene would vanish. The hatred with which those two little optical men hurled themselves at each other filled me with horror. I couldn't stand it, and so made them dissolve by popping open my eyes, reducing the scene to a quick sketch of an unarmed thrust. What happened next? I never found out, but perhaps one day I will.

The performance was on Saturday, late afternoon. I cut short by a little—a very little—my session at the pool, showered, and took a brief nap. I went downstairs after they telephoned me to say that the bus was ready to leave.

My colleagues, both men and women, were all dressed in their Sunday best, as if they were going to the opera. The young female students—conference volunteers—wore fancy outfits, and their dark, heavily made-up faces were crowned by high, elaborate hairdos, topped with silk bows. Two buses were waiting, as well as a long line of taxis and limousines. As always, we were running late. I got on the first bus, whose driver was impatiently honking the horn, and we shot off. To save time, we took the highway that circled the city, and the whole way I contemplated the view of the mountains through my window, absorbed in my own thoughts. If my calculations were correct, that very night the final gong would sound as my cloning machine completed its task and the Genius hatched from his shell. Creation's integuments were undoubtedly already expanding. At dawn, the finished clone of Carlos Fuentes would be making its way down the mountain, and thus the final phase of my Great Work would commence.

At the airport everything was ready for the show, which began as soon as the last invited guests arrived. Though they had reserved a seat for me in the front row, I preferred to watch it from further back, standing up, hidden—one could say—"in the wings," that is, behind the plants, because the show was being staged in a garden surrounded by waiting gates, ticket counters, and the bar of the glass-enclosed pre-boarding area. It was a marvelous garden, though somewhat wild; at those latitudes it is difficult to keep vegetation under control. Bushes with flame-like flowers surrounded the palm trees, the banyan tree spread its eavelike branches in all directions, the fern fronds formed dense screens, and everywhere hung enormous yellow, violet, and blue orchids. The leaves of some of the plants were so large that one was enough for me to hide behind. I enjoyed spying on the audience. Everyone looked like automatons from the very heart of my experiments. I underwent some kind of doubling of the self. I thought: "If they were real, what would they be doing right now?" But the other part of me knew they were real. It was as if reality itself had switched time frames and one had leapt into another ... Years ago, in this same place, I had seen Amelina for the last time, we'd said our final parting words, replete with tears and promises. This spot remained pregnant, like objective rapture. I realized I was looking for her but wouldn't see her. How to see through the walls of the present? The garden's exuberance, transparent in its repetition, was reflected in the buildings' enormous panes of glass, and through those ghostly labyrinths passed the airplanes' huge white forms.

It may have had something to do with the time of day. The sun had dropped behind the mountains, which were so high and so close, thereby causing confusion. After disappearing from the sky, the sun's golden glow in the atmosphere intensified.

The moment the first lines of dialogue were spoken—which I remembered better than I would have wanted to—things got stranger. My eyes were drawn, as if magnetically, to Carlos Fuentes, sitting in the front row.

I saw he was absorbed in the play, totally focused, trans-
ported to another world. By his side sat his wife, Sylvia,
as beautiful as the good fairy of storybook fame, looking
relaxed and with a vague smile of interest playing on her
lips. Authorial vanity, which never completely fell away,
not even at that moment, made me wonder what they
would think of my little play. I feared I would come up
short in their estimation. But, I told myself, this was inevitable, and anyway, what did it matter at this point?

The laughter surprised me. I had forgotten that an audience could react. I quickly turned my attention back to
the actors, who were evolving in the middle of the garden. Eve was lying on a divan, wearing a cumbersome red
sultana's dress and holding in her arms a rubber Mickey
Mouse doll. She seemed to be waiting for something with
great impatience. Two jesters played on harps at her feet.
A servant entered and announced:

"Mr. Adam can't come right now. He's busy."

What was all this about? I didn't recognize it, it was
too Dadaist. Nevertheless, I had written it. Eve went to
his laboratory to get him. Adam agreed to have tea with
her, but not to put down his Exoscope, an enormous instrument he carried around with great difficulty. Slowly,
I began to remember. Yes, I had written that. Moreover,
they were scrupulously following the text, to the very last
comma. Gone were any remaining doubts that I had written it, for there were my recurrent themes, my little tricks,
and even the dialogues I had lifted verbatim from reality
and that carried me back to teas I'd had with my wife on

long-ago summer afternoons. But why were they drinking from such oversized five-gallon cups? At that point, I had to remember (which I did) my mental process while I was writing; in this case, remembering meant reconstructing. That detail about the cups meant to suggest that at the beginning of the world there was still no congruency in the sizes of things: this had required a much longer span of evolution. The dialogues, spoken with a Caribbean accent, sounded strange to me, especially when I began to recall their intellectual pulse, but I had to admit they were verbatim.

There was only one innovation in this production: Adam was black. Though this didn't exactly qualify as an innovation. The actor was black, and he was probably the best actor they had. They weren't about to discriminate against him! In Venezuela there are lots of blacks, though many fewer in the Andean region, and even fewer at the university. Those there are tend to be outstanding, so it shouldn't have surprised me that they had given him the main role. They probably pretended he was just another actor, like any of the others, and, to tell the truth, I was probably the only one who realized he was black.

As for the Exoscope Adam carried around with him throughout the entire play, they had, indeed, done a good job, even though they resorted to the simplest and most unimaginative solution. The entire play pivoted on this instrument. In the notes, I had specified only its size (six-and-a-half feet by five feet by three-and-a-half feet, more or less) and that it should look like a scientific-optical device. The idea, which the props person had understood, was that it would be a celibate machine; perhaps he had understood it a little too well, because this Exoscope looked a lot like Duchamp's *Large Glass*.

The plot unfolded one event at a time. The entire drama was based on the mysterious impossibility nested at the very heart of the relationship between the two protagonists. Their love was real, but at the same time it was impossible. Adam's experiments, Eve's courtesan frivolities, all were mere evasions. Love was revealed as an impossibility that seemed either metaphysical or supernatural, but was in reality very simple and even prosaic: Adam was married.

I must confess, I didn't know how to resolve the difficult problem this plot line presented. Because if Adam and Eve were, respectively, the only man and the only woman on the planet, then Adam's wife—the absent wife whose existence prevented him from living out his love with Eve—couldn't be anybody other than Eve herself. The idea (very characteristic of me, to the point that I believe it to be how I conceive of literature) had been to create something equivalent to those figures that was both realistic and impossible, like Escher's *Belvedere*, figures that look viable in a drawing but could not be built because they are but an illusion of perspective. Such a thing can be written, but one must be very inspired, very focused. I fail because of my precipitousness, my rush to finish, and my desperation to please. I was able to sustain it in this play only through the strength of ambiguities and funny repartees. And only for a short time, because very soon things started to happen.

It was then, when the action rushed toward a resolution, after the exasperating teatime dialogues, that the extent of my fiasco fell on me like a mental atomic bomb. Once again I had submitted to nonsense, to the frivolity of invention for invention's sake, resorting to the unexpected as if it were some kind of deus ex machina! Again I had squandered the wise ancient advice adorning the frontispiece of my literary ethic, "Simplify, my son, simplify!" I have managed to write a few good things by following, quite by accident, that advice. What a waste! Only through minimalism is it possible to achieve the asymmetry that for me is the flower of art; complications inevitably form heavy symmetries, which are vulgar and overwrought.

But my mania—to be constantly adding things, episodes, characters, paragraphs, to be constantly veering off course, branching out—is fatal. It must be due to insecurity, fear that the basics are not enough, so I have to keep adding more and more adornment until I achieve a kind of surrealist rococo, which exasperates me more than it does anybody else.

It was like a nightmare (the mother of all nightmares) to watch the living defects of what I had written materialize in front of me. Though my punishment was a kind of poetic justice, because from that point on the logic the play began to obey was the logic of nightmares. Poor Adam's brain began to rebel against him, and in a burst of dementia he murdered Eve … The scene was full of gruesome details: he decapitated her, and, after performing a few macabre juggling acts with her head, he divided her long blond hair into two locks and tied them around the waist of the corpse, which he left standing. The hair knot hung over her buttocks, and her head hung down in front of her sex, like a codpiece ... then he ran off, still carrying the Exoscope. The police of Babylon got involved, and the inspector in charge proclaimed: We are dealing with a serial killer, there is a pattern, this is the seventh such crime, all with long blond hair, all with the head tied around the waist ... But Adam, by definition, was the first and only man! Therefore, he couldn't be just one among many suspects, he was by necessity the guilty party. And moreover, if Eve were the only woman, how could she be one in a series of victims? Serial killers came later in evolution. I myself didn't even understand it.

In the next scene, in the cave where Adam went to hide, Eve's ghost appeared as an integral part of the glass of the celibate machine. Agents of a foreign power took advantage of the situation to steal the Exoscope from him, without knowing that Eve continued to live inside it ... It was grotesque, repulsive; I was mortified.

VII

Difficult as it is to believe, people liked that crap. It was nighttime by the time it ended. In the last light of day, at the culminating moment of the show, the evening flight arrived; there are two flights a day to Mérida, and both have to land during daylight hours because of how difficult it is to land a plane in this narrow valley surrounded by high peaks. The noise of the engines drowned out a few lines, and shortly thereafter the passengers walked in single file across the stage carrying their bags and suitcases but without interrupting the show. That detail was the most widely discussed during the reception hosted afterward by the airport director. There was a festive atmosphere, almost euphoric; everybody seemed happy, except me. I allowed myself to carry out the bad idea of drinking myself out of my depression. Since my detoxification, ten years earlier, I had not had a drop of alcohol. At least I had the good sense not to mix my drinks, but rum is deceptive, always so smooth, so calming, like a perennial cause with no effect, until the effect shows itself, and then you realize the effect had been there from the beginning, even before there began to be a cause. The hall had a bad echo. Everybody was shouting and nobody could hear anybody else. I accepted the congratulations with the graciousness of a perfect idiot. I watched lips move and smiles appear, sometimes I moved my lips, too, and drank, and smiled again; my face was hurting from holding that grimace for so long. That was even how I received Carlos Fuentes's words.

What happened next is blurred by the fog of intoxication. We boarded buses that took us directly to the hotel dining room for dinner, from there we went to the bar so we could keep drinking, and at midnight we took taxis to a discotheque ... Throughout the many stages of that night I felt, underneath the strong effects of the rum, a discomfort that never let up, undoubtedly because I never managed to put my finger on what it was. I didn't know what was wrong; it couldn't be that I felt out of place, because that was normal for me. In retrospect, I understood what was happening to me: in my semiconscious state I had joined the group of young people: I returned with them on the bus, sat with them at dinner, and continued in their company through all that followed. They were the students who did volunteer work (they called it "logistics") for the convention, almost all of them female, almost none older than twenty. People who signed up for this were not necessarily devotees of literature. My colleagues had done nothing to extricate me from them, on the contrary. They were corroborating the reputation I had forged for myself of preferring "life" to literature. They were convinced that I was pursuing the young women, and they approved; in a certain way it legitimized them indirectly by showing that literature was part of life and passion. As far as the students were concerned, they asked for nothing more than the attention I seemed to be paying them, the fact that I chose them over the famous writers I should have been interacting with, and the chance to be seen in public with the hero of the Macuto Line.

I spent the rest of the night at the discotheque. There were strobe lights, blasting salsa music, and so many people you could hardly move. But I didn't care, I was in the stratosphere. The young people were my drunken bodyguards. The erroneous impression my more mature colleagues got of me could have been seen from a different point of view, which in the end was the same: vampirism. My false maturity could not be seen in any other way. But my vampirism is special, I think.

Vampirism is the key to my relationships with others, the only mechanism that allows me to interact. Of course, this is a metaphor. Vampires, as such, do not exist, they are merely a hook on which to hang all manner of shameful parasitisms that need metaphor to come to terms with themselves. The shape that metaphor takes in me is special, as I said. What I need—which I suck from the other—is neither money, nor security, nor admiration, nor, in professional terms, subject matter or stories. It is style. I have discovered that every human being, every living being in reality, in addition to everything he has to show for himself by way of material and spiritual possessions, has a style he uses to manage those possessions. And I have learned to detect it and appropriate it. Which

has important consequences for my relationships, at least
for those I have established since I turned forty: they are
temporary, they begin and end, and they are quite fleeting,
more and more fleeting as I become increasingly skilled
at capturing another's personal style. Any other kind of
vampirism could lead to permanent relationships; for example, if I extracted money or attention from my victim,
the other's reserves would likely become infinite. Even if I
were looking for stories, a single subject could supply me
indefinitely. But not style. It has a mechanism that gets
worn out in the interpersonal transfer. Once in action, I
watch my victim quickly dry up, wilted and vacant, and I
lose all interest. Then I move on to the next one.

I have now revealed the entire secret of my scientific activity. My famous clones are nothing more than the dupli-
cation of style cells. Which should lead me to question my
appetite for styles. I think the answer resides in the mere
necessity to persist. I have sought an outlet for this need
through love, without any success, so far.

We were crowded together on a bench pushed against
a wall; next to me, at moments talking to me, sat Nelly,
one of my young Venezuelan friends, a graduate student
in literature. I admired her and I had a tendency to feel toward her that rare kind of envy that crosses sexual barri-
ers. She must have been twenty-one or twenty-two, but
she was the embodiment of an ageless ideal. She was small
and thin, her features were unusually pure, and she had
enormous eyes and an aristocratic air. Her suit—wide
pants and bustier—was made of brown satin; her perfect
breasts were almost exposed; she wore very pointy Asian

slippers on her feet. Her blond curly hair fell over her shoulders at an angle, covering one eye. Part of her charm lay in her incongruity. She was mulatto, perhaps also with some indigenous blood, but her face was French. Her hair color was recent, judging by the comments I heard from her friends; I had met her as a redhead, years before. One could never guess what she was thinking. In the discotheque she was calm, relaxed, a glass of rum in her hand, her beautiful eyes lost in contemplation. She seemed to be elsewhere. She spoke only when spoken to; when not, she allowed a peaceful, cozy silence to envelop her. She spoke in a whisper, but she articulated her words so well that I could understand her perfectly over the loud music.

"You are enchanting tonight, Nelly," I told her, my tongue heavy with alcohol. "As usual, I should say. Or did I already say that? Every sentence I utter comes out twice, though that's why I feel it twice as strongly, wrapped as it is in the deep truth of its meaning and its intention."

For a moment she seemed not to have heard me, but that was her usual reaction. In that minuscule space between our two bodies, she turned toward me, like the statue of a goddess turning on the altar.

"I dressed up especially in your honor, César. Today is your day."

"Thank you very much. I am enjoying it. But you are always elegant, it's a part of you."

"That's kind of you to say so. You are good inside and out, César." My face must have betrayed my puzzlement at the second statement, because I heard her add, "You are young and beautiful."

The lights were very low, we were practically in the dark. Or rather, the beams and pulses of the colored lights allowed us to see what was going on but not reconstruct it in our minds. This is the astute discovery such night spots have made. Their lighting arrangements reproduce subjectivity thereby nullifying it, a process further assisted by the alcohol and the noise. From the depths of this nullification rose, golden and warm like a houri out of paradise, the beautiful Nelly. I slipped my arm around her waist and kissed her. Her lips had a strange flavor, which made me think of the taste of silk. We were so close, so nearly on top of each other, that every gesture we made required only minimal displacement—almost imperceptible.

"I am no longer young," I told her. "Haven't you noticed how much hair I've lost since my last visit?"

She looked at my hair and shook her head. I insisted with the obstinacy of a drunk. I told her that my imminent baldness terrified me. And it wasn't just out of vanity; there was a very concrete reason. I told her that when I was young I shaved my head in a rapture of madness, then had a message tattooed on my scalp, which my hair then covered when it grew back. If I went bald and this inscription were revealed, it would be the end of the scant prestige I had managed to build up as a fragile defensive shield around me.

"Why? What does it say?" she asked, pretending for a moment that she believed me.

"I can only tell you that it is a declaration of belief in the existence of extraterrestrials."

A violet light that swept fleetingly over her face showed

me her serious smile.

That was why, I went on to explain, I spent a fortune on shampoos with capillary nutrients, and why, not trusting commercial products, I had dedicated my life to chemistry.

A while later, changing the subject, I asked about the ring she was wearing on her left hand. It was a fascinating piece of jewelry, shaped like a crown, with a blue stone whose facets seemed to have been set separately. She told me it was her graduation ring, one of the traditions of the university, though hers had a special feature: they had doubled hers in honor of her having earned two simultaneous degrees, as Professor of Literature and Professor of the Teaching of Literature; it was a fairly subtle distinction, but she seemed quite proud of this double achievement.

She left her silky hand between my paws corroded by the nucleic acid I work with. I lifted it to my eyes so I could examine the ring, which was truly a notable piece for its workmanship and clever design. Each time a ball of strobe light rolled over us, the blue stone lit up brilliantly, and through the two tiny chiseled windows I could see the crowd of young people dancing. The thin gold ribbon that twisted around the stone carried an inscription.

"Look," she said turning the ring around with two fingers from her other hand. "Can you see how the words of the inscription recombine to form other words, spelling out both of my two degrees?"

I couldn't, of course, due to the lack of light and my befuddlement at that late hour, but I could admire the mechanism. I kissed those fingers.

May God forgive me, but I began to doubt the seriousness of the course of studies at that tropical university.
All those exchanges and caresses in that discotheque were
part of a larger context through which I was taking a measure of Nelly's true intelligence. All my seductive moves,
both the innocent and the daring, and even the most im-
passioned and sincere, have in common the same back-
drop: my constant evaluation of the intelligence of the
woman in question. I can't help it. Even further in the
background must be my adolescent fantasy of having a
sex slave, a woman who submits, without any reserve, to
the will of my desire. For this, her intelligence must have
a very special size and configuration. But intelligence is
mysterious. It always gets the better of me, escapes my
manipulations—even my literary ones—and remains an
insolvable enigma.

I was interested in Nelly for another reason, both more
positive and more ineffable. She was Amelina's best
friend, her confidante, she knew everything about her ...
Among other things she knew where she was hiding. She
was in on the secret, though secretive herself, thereby establishing a continuum of love. The two women weren't
at all alike, they were almost opposites. Once I had com-
pared them, in jest, to the sun and the moon. There in
the disco, in my intoxicated state, I had next to me, throb-
bing and perfect, a reality that touched all other realities
and spread through them until it encompassed the entire
world. Nelly's dreamy eyes lost themselves in the night
and in me.

VIII

At dawn, things emerged from their reality, as if in a drop of water. The most trivial objects, embellished with profound reality, made me quiver almost painfully. A tuft of grass, a paving stone, a scrap of cloth, everything was soft and dense. We were in the Plaza Bolívar, as lush and leafy as a real forest. The sky had turned blue, not a cloud in sight, no stars or airplanes, as if emptied of everything; the sun should have appeared from behind the mountains, but its rays were not yet touching even the highest peak to the west. The light intensified and bodies projected no shadows. The dark and the light floated in layers. The birds didn't sing, the insects must have been asleep, the trees remained as still as in a painting. And, at my feet, the real kept being born, like a mineral being born atom by atom.

The strangeness that made everything sparkle came from me. Worlds rose out of my bottomless perplexity.

"So, am I capable of love?" I asked myself. "Can I really love truly, like in a soap opera, like in reality?" The question surpassed the thinkable. Love? Me, love? Me, the brain man, the aesthete of the intellect? Wouldn't something need to happen to make it possible, some cosmic sign, an event that would turn the course of events around, an eclipse of a kind…? Inches away from my shoe, one more atom crystallized in a blaze of transparency, then another… If I could love, just like that, without the universe getting turned upside down, the only persistent condition that made reality real was contiguity: that things were next to things, in rows or on plates… No, it was impossible, I couldn't believe it. Nevertheless… Plop! Another atom of air, in front of my face, initiating another spiral of splendid combustion. If all conditions can be reduced to a single condition, it is this: Adam and Eve were real.

Nelly and I, sitting on a stone bench under the trees, were as pale as a sheet of paper. My features were as drawn as could be, an old man's face, pale, bloodless, my hair sticking out. I knew this because I was looking at my reflection in the glass of the Exoscope we had in front of us. The actors of the University Theatre had brought it to the disco at the end of the party, to pay me a goodbye homage; we danced around it like savages enacting a rain dance, watching our reflections in miniature and upside down. Afterward, drunk as they were, they left it behind, and I made the effort to carry it to the plaza, thinking that sooner or later they would remember it and come get it—they needed it for the show's official opening.

I had to admit they had done a good job. The dawn was fully reflected in the Exoscope, and in that dawn, the two of us, as if after the end of the world. With great effort I turned my eyes away from the instrument's glass and looked directly at Nelly. Without knowing why, I asked her a stupid question.

"What are you thinking about?"

She remained quiet but alert for a moment, her eyes lost in the void.

"Do you hear that, César? What's going on?"

I could have sworn the silence was absolute, though as a foreigner I was unable to determine what was normal or abnormal within that silence. In any case, it was not the silence that was puzzling Nelly. Awakening from my reverie, I heard shouts of alarm, cars suddenly accelerating, sirens, all in a kind of dull buzz that pulsated around me, still not disturbing the otherworldly peace of the city center, though approaching.

"The birds have stopped singing," Nelly whispered, "even the flies have gone into hiding."

"Could it be an earthquake?" I ventured.

"Could be," she said noncommittally.

A car drove past the plaza at full speed. Behind it came a military truck full of armed soldiers, one of whom saw us and shouted something, but they were driving so fast we couldn't understand him.

"Look!" Nelly shouted, pointing up.

I looked up and saw a crowd of people on the roof terrace of a building, all staring off into the distance and shouting. The same thing was happening on the balconies of the other buildings around that plaza. Right in front of us the cathedral bells began to ring. In a flash the streets were thronging with cars filled with entire families … It seemed like collective madness. As far as I was concerned, it might have been normal: I didn't know the customs of that city, and nothing precluded this from being what happened every Sunday at dawn: the locals coming out onto their balconies and terraces to check the weather, and shouting out joyfully that it was a beautiful day for their outings and sporting events; the cathedral bells, for their part, calling people to morning services; families leaving early for their picnics ... If I hadn't been with Nelly I could have taken it as the normal Sunday routine. But she was extremely puzzled, and even a bit alarmed.

It was obvious that whatever was happening was happening far away, and far away in this small, enclosed valley meant the surrounding mountains. We couldn't see them from the plaza, but there were panoramic views from any of the adjacent streets, one of the city's great tourist attractions. I stood up. Nelly must have been thinking the same thing because she also got up and quickly figured out the closest spot where we could find out what was happening.

"Let's go to the archway on Humboldt Street," she said, already starting off. That archway, which I was familiar with, was about one hundred yards away; it stood at the foot of a very long public stairway that was so steep you could see half the valley from there. I started to follow her, then stopped her with my hand.

"Should we leave this monstrosity here?" I asked, pointing to the Exoscope.

She shrugged. We left it and walked off quickly. In the

César Aira

brief time it took us to get to the archway, just a short distance away, the activity in the streets had increased so much it was difficult to make our way through the crowds. Everybody was nervous, some were terrified, most were rushing around as if their lives depended on it. Everyone was talking, but I couldn't understand a word, as if they were speaking foreign languages, which must be a natural effect of panic.

When we got there, we saw it. It was so astonishing it took a while for me to absorb. To begin with, we saw that the alarm was justified, to say the least. I don't know exactly how to describe it. At first, it was otherworldly; it was still dawn, the sun hadn't yet appeared, the sky was very clear and very empty, bodies projected no shadows ... and colossal blue worms were slowly descending from the mountain peaks ... I'm aware that stating it like this might bring automatic writing to mind, but stating it is my only choice. It seems like the insertion of a different plot line, from an old B-rated science fiction movie, for example. Nevertheless, the seamless continuity had at no time been interrupted. They were living beings, of this I was certain: I had too much experience manipulating life forms to make that mistake. There are some movements no machine can imitate. I calculated the size of the worms: they were approximately one thousand feet long and seventy feet in diameter; they were almost perfect cylinders, with no heads or tails, although their geometric form had to be mentally reconstructed because they were coiling and twisting and changing shape as they moved across the anfractuous mountain terrain. They also looked soft and slimy, but their formidable weight could be deduced by observing them displace enormous rocks along their way, sunder the mountainside, and reduce whole trees to splinters. The most extraordinary thing, which would have been worthy of admiration had the circumstances not added an extra touch of terror, was their color: a phosphorescent blue with watery tones, like an almost darkened sky, a blue that seemed dampened by fresh placentas.

Nelly grabbed my arm. She was horrified. I swept my eyes along the perimeter of this great Andean amphitheater: there were hundreds of worms, all descending toward the city. From the shouts, which I quickly began to understand, I learned that the same thing was occurring in the mountains behind us, the ones we couldn't see from where we stood. I've already said that Mérida is completely surrounded by mountains. This meant only one thing: very soon we would be crushed by the monsters. The landslides they were provoking were cataclysmic; the entire valley shook as stones the size of houses tumbled down the slopes, and there was probably already vast destruction on the outskirts. A simple projected calculation revealed that the city was doomed. Two or three of these worms would be enough to leave no brick standing. And there were hundreds of them! Moreover, with horror and despair I realized that the quantity was indefinite ... and increasing. It was as if they kept being born, and the process showed no signs of stopping.

The ones in front were already halfway between the

highest peaks and the valley floor. That's why they were descending: their own multiplication was forcing them downhill. It was an almost mechanical destiny, not one due to any murderous impulse on the part of these strange beasts. In fact, they were much too strange to harbor any agenda. Their size was what would destroy us … If anyone entertained a hope that their size was an optical illusion, and that they would get smaller as they descended until they appeared as inoffensive as cigarette butts under the soles of our shoes, they would have to dismiss the idea: they were very real, and having one nearby would be a terminal experience.

Any hope regarding the relativity of their size was painfully dispelled a few minutes later, when we witnessed the following episode from where we were standing under the archway. Several military trucks, the one we had seen driving past the plaza and others, converged on a road that rose in the direction of the worms. We saw them stop when they reached the one nearest the city. The soldiers got out and fanned out in front of the blue mass. At that moment denial was no longer possible: the men looked like insects next to the monster—and pathetically ineffectual. This became obvious once they began to shoot at it with their machine guns. They didn't miss their target once (it was like aiming at the mountain itself), but they could have continued for an eternity to the same effect, that is, to no effect. The bullets disappeared into the soft tons of blue flesh like pebbles tossed into the sea. They tried bazookas, cannons, hand grenades, even antiaircraft missiles fired from the hood of one of the trucks, all with the same derisive futility. The climax came when the worm, in the course of its blind march, slid down a steep slope and one section of its body rolled onto the road, crushing trucks and men like an enormous rolling pin, reducing them to laminas. The survivors ran off in terror. The crowd broke their awed silence as they watched the events unfold, and I heard cries and shouts of anguish. Their worst fears were being confirmed. Somebody pointed to another spot, to one side, where another catastrophe was taking place: it was the highway that led across the plateau and out of the valley. Another worm had fallen over a compact line of cars trying to escape, causing innumerable fatalities. Traffic came to a standstill, and people abandoned their cars and ran between the rocks and bushes back toward the city. There was no escape. This was definitive. Eyes turned with fear toward the old colonial buildings around us: the city itself seemed to be the last possible refuge, and it was an illusion to think that its feeble walls could withstand the weight of the worms.

The collective attention turned back to itself, as if to confirm the reality of what was occurring through the reaction of fear. And I was implicated in this reversion. Like so many others, like everybody, perhaps, I have always thought that in a real collective catastrophe I would find the material of my dreams, take it in hand, shape it, finally; then, even if only for an instant, everything would be permitted. It would take something as grand and widespread as an earthquake, an interplanetary collision, or a war to make the circumstances genuinely objective and thus make room for my subjectivity to take hold of the reins of action.

But the subjective was made manifest even in the supremely objective. The examples of cataclysms hereby offered, which in reality are not examples, do not include the invasion of enormous slimy creatures. That would never happen in real life; it rises out of a feverish imagination, in this case mine, and returns to it as a metaphor for my private life.

Here I have again reached the moment to change levels, to make another "translation." But this one is so radical that it comes full circle and reties the plot line exactly where I left it.

The mental process of the character representing me in the previous "translation," from the point at which he was contemplating the benefits of a collective catastrophe, apparently dissolved entirely into fiction, then gathered up all the loose ends and elaborated a generalized reinterpretation, not only of the previous "translations" but of the process itself out of which "translations" arise.

Just as when interpreting a nightmare, I was assailed by a sudden doubt: might it be my fault? A priori, this seemed absurd, an extreme manifestation—exaggerated to the point of caricature—of the lack of proportion between small causes and grand effects. But one thing led to the next, and in a vertiginous process this conjecture became more and more plausible. I went back and reviewed my own "translations" until I found the root of them all, the device from which they had emerged. In my mind, the march of the worms became retrograde, and with the same brutal blindness with which they were descending, they turned and climbed back up, destroying my inventions, from whose crushed cadavers rose little clouds of memory, ghosts of memory.

Because I had forgotten everything. The same system that created my thoughts took charge of erasing them, turning them into sinuous white strips that reached across every level. How can there be so much amnesia in a single lifetime? Isn't this a point in favor of the theory of reincarnation?

Of course, there is such a thing as "blind translation," the act of mechanically transposing one language to another, without passing through the content, which is what professional translators do when they come across a technical and detailed description of a machine or a process … In order to understand what it's about, they would need to consult a manual on the subject, study something they know nothing about and doesn't interest them … But that isn't necessary! By translating correctly, sentence by sentence, the entire page, the translation will turn out well, they will continue to be as happily ignorant as they were at the beginning, and they will get paid for their work. After all, they are paid to know the language, not the subject matter.

The inverted vortex of the titanic herd of blue worms was located somewhere in the mountains. They emerged from that spot into the light and began to slither—even before they came fully into view—along the broken horizon of the peaks, like a ball circling the top of the roulette wheel, until they stopped, made their appearance, and began to descend. There were so many and their issuance was so constant that they were all descending at once from all points around the circle (in that particular game of roulette, all the numbers came up at once). I could pinpoint the locus of their emergence, and I was the only person who could: it was the cloning machine. It couldn't be anything else. The years I had devoted full time to the manipulation of cloned materials had so refined my sixth sense that I could recognize it. These worms had all the characteristics; their very excess—where would that come from if not the uncontrolled multiplication of cells that only the cloning machine could generate? Functional beings have inviolable limits. My first thought was that the machine was malfunctioning, had gone haywire. But I immediately corrected myself; that thought was worthy only of a citizen of a consumer society who buys a microwave or a video camera and is overwhelmed by its complexity. This was not the case with me, because I had invented the cloning machine, and nobody knew better than I that it was infallibly rational.

As I have already mentioned, the worms' color and texture were their most noticeable characteristics. They are also what led me to the heart of the matter. Because that color, that very peculiar brilliant blue, immediately reminded me of the color of Carlos Fuentes's cell, which my wasp had brought me ... Though when I saw that color in the cell it did not evoke what it was evoking now that I was seeing it extended over vast undulating surfaces. I now realized I had seen that same color somewhere else, the very same day the cell had been taken, one week before. Where? On the tie Carlos Fuentes was wearing that day! A splendid Italian raw silk tie, over an immaculate white shirt ... and a light grey suit ... (one memory led to another until the picture was complete). And this horrendous piece of evidence revealed the magnitude of the error. The wasp had brought me a cell from Carlos Fuentes's *tie*, not his body. A groan escaped my lips.

"Stupid wasp and the accursed mother who made you!"

"What?" Nelly asked, surprised.

"Don't pay any attention to me, I understand myself."

The fact is, I couldn't blame her. It was all my fault. How could that poor disposable cloned tool know where the man stopped and his clothing began? For her it was all one, it was all "Carlos Fuentes." After all, it was no different than what happened when the critics and professors who were attending the conference found it difficult to say where the man ended and his books began; for them, too, all of it was "Carlos Fuentes."

I saw it with the clarity of the noonday sun: the silk cell contained the DNA of the worm that had produced it, and the cloning machine, functioning perfectly, had done nothing more than decode and recode the information, with the results we were now witnessing. The blue monsters were nothing more nor less than silkworm clones, and if they had been magnified to that absurd size it was simply because I had set the cloning machine to run in "genius" mode. Under other circumstances I would have smiled with melancholic irony upon seeing to what awkward and destructive gigantism literary greatness could be reduced when it was passed through the weave and warp of life.

I came to my senses after having lost myself in thoughts that rushed through me like a hiccup, and I felt an urgency to do something, anything, to prevent the imminent catastrophe. Regrettably, I have no talent for improvisation. But this was the time for action, not regrets. I would think of something. And even if I didn't, everything would turn out well. If I had started it, I could end it. If it had come out of me, it had to return to me. It couldn't be that I would be responsible for the deaths of several tens of thousands of innocent people and the utter devastation—no stone would remain standing—of this old city. The very possibility of the disaster cast over my being a demonic splendor. In my role as a writer, I am inoffensive. What more could I want than to be diabolical, a destroyer of worlds?! But it is impossible. Well reasoned, however, therein lie the benefits of the changes in level, because then I could, in reality, be a diabolical being, an evil monster: such things are fairly relative, as everyone knows from daily experience.

I grabbed Nelly by the shoulder, and we left the group under the archway. The entire crowd was dispersing, women and men moving suddenly and without any apparent purpose. What could they do? Hide in a cellar? Make final arrangements? In the end, they had to do something.

Nelly was in shock. I brought my face up to hers and spoke to provoke a response from her.

"I'm going to do something. I think I can stop them." She looked at me incredulously. I repeated, "If anyone can save the city, I can."

"But, how?" she stammered, looking behind her.

"You're going to have to help me," which wasn't altogether true, among other reasons because I still hadn't devised a plan. But it worked, her eyes recovered a glimmer of interest. She must have remembered that I was the hero of the Macuto Line and that performing feats of historical proportion was not unknown to me.

We didn't have to go far. We literally bumped into an empty car that had its motor running and the door open; its owner must have joined the group watching events from the archway.

"Let's go!" I said. I got in behind the wheel. Nelly sat in the passenger seat. We drove off. It was a taxi, an old Pontiac from the seventies, as long and wide as only cars in Venezuela can be today.

I feared the streets would be blocked, but they weren't. The paralysis of uncertainty persisted throughout the city. I sped up, and we came to Viaduct Avenue. The only solution I could think of was to find a way through the newborn beasts, reach the cloning machine, and turn it off. In this way at least I could stop their emergence. I didn't know if putting the machine in reverse would reabsorb the worms, but I could try. In the meantime, I stepped on the gas. We were soon on the viaduct, where we commanded an excellent view of the blue masses slithering down the mountains.

"Where are we going?" Nelly asked. "I don't think we can escape."

"That is not my intention, quite the contrary. I'm going to try to get to the place where they are coming from," at which point I inserted a tiny white lie, because I didn't want her to guess that I was responsible for the disaster. "What we have to do is close the … hole they are coming out of, and perhaps make them go back … underground."

She believed me. It was absurd, but in a certain way it evoked the spring mechanism of the Macuto Line, over which I had already been triumphant, and this lent it a patina of truth.

I kept climbing, driving faster and faster. The old Pontiac vibrated, its panels rattling. Driving helped me recuperate some of my lost coordination; a sleepless night and the alcohol had left every cell in my body dead tired. I was overwhelmed with exhaustion. But the internal adrenalin bath sustained my movements, and slowly I recovered my faculties.

I turned left onto a small, very steep street, shifted into first gear, and floored the gas until the motor roared. In a final effort the clunker carried us onto the highway that circled the city. I turned right, moving in the same direction as the morning breeze; snakes and rats, escaping in terror from the mountains, were scrambling across the asphalt. We could now see from close up what was happening. The blue of the worms filled the windshield. They were everywhere, nearby and far away, and their forward march was inexorable. The route we were taking would be quite dangerous in a matter of minutes, and if not, would become so later on. We heard a few rocks, luckily quite small, falling on the roof of the car. I began to doubt the feasibility of my plan. Reaching the cloning machine seemed like mission impossible. We would have to abandon the car sooner or later, perhaps quite soon; I hoped to drive at least as far as the intersection with the road that continued along the plateau; but I remembered that I had climbed on foot for an hour or more before setting down the machine. And based on the way events were unfolding, this interval would give the worms plenty of time to turn the city into a tabula rasa. That is, if we managed to avoid them and reach our goal. We passed by one that was slithering down the hill about two hundred yards from the road. Seen from close up, they were overwhelming. Their shape, which from far away had seemed so well defined, so worm-like, here turned into a blue mess, cloudlike. Nelly devoured it all with her eyes, in silence. She turned to look back at the city, as if calculating the time left before the inevitable occurred. At that moment I sensed she was remembering something, and, in fact, she let out a choked exclamation and looked at me.

"César!"

"What?" I said, lifting my foot off the gas pedal.

"I forgot about Amelina!"

This surprise completely confused me. At that moment more than ever before, Amelina felt like a myth, the legend of love. I had already resigned myself to never seeing her again, so her name came to me from a distance that was purely linguistic. But Nelly's words carried with them an urgency of reality that forced me to adopt a more practical perspective, as if Amelina really did exist. And, undoubtedly, she did. She was somewhere in the city we saw spread out to our right, small and threatened like the model of a city in the hands of an angry child. The image of Florencia, my childhood love, flitted through my mind, the young and enamored Florencia, whom I felt had been reborn in Amelina thirty years later. Like in a trick diorama, what was far away looked close and vice versa. Love's ghostly stand-ins, which had shaped my life, were spinning around me, forming a tunnel of black light that I was sinking into.

"Where is she?"

"At her house. She sleeps late and very heavily. We must go wake her up and tell her what's going on!"

What good would that do her? None, of course. And us, even less. But the idea attracted me for two reasons: first, I could see Amelina again, and under savage and peremptory circumstances; second, it was the perfect excuse to abandon my impractical plan of reaching the cloning machine. The very instant I made the decision to go, I became possessed by an almost infantile euphoria, because Nelly's words implied that Amelina still lived alone, she had not gotten married, and she, Nelly, continued to think of her in relation to me, and if she had decided to mention her only under this extremity, it was because our love story was real, it carried across all the translations, it would keep its appointment ...

"Let's go," I said. "But you'll have to guide me."

She pointed to the first exit, and I veered off the highway, making the tires screech. We turned our backs on the mountain and the worms, as if to say, "Who cares!" and we returned to the city along a road I didn't know. She told me that Amelina was still living in one of the student apartments in the Nancy Building, the same one where I had visited her years before. It wasn't far away, but nothing was in such a small city.

The traffic got heavier, though it was still moving because nobody was paying any attention to the traffic lights. I wondered where they were all going. From the terraces, people kept looking toward the mountains with the same expectations, the same alarm, the same dismay. They were not taking any measures, but what could they do? The cars were driving like crazy, all in the same direction...

"Where are they going?" Nelly asked.

Suddenly, I knew: to the airport. It seemed strange that I hadn't thought of that sooner; apparently others had. The only way out was by air. But, even assuming there were still some private airplanes available and that military planes were on their way, many could not be saved, let alone all. The commercial flight arrived at ten and departed at eleven, if they hadn't cancelled it. And if it arrived full of passengers, the passengers themselves would want to remain on the flight back to Caracas.

A Mercedes Benz, its horn blasting like a siren, passed us; I glimpsed Carlos Fuentes and his wife in the back seat, their profiles set in serious expressions. They, too, were on their way to the airport. How naive! Or, perhaps, they had been offered seats on an official plane? The city was the provincial capital, and surely the governor would have one ... but I found it hard to believe that in this predicament of "save yourself if you can," literary hierarchies would be respected. No way! Surely they were going to try to somehow wangle a seat, like so many others ... I remembered that I had a reservation for the eleven o'clock flight, I was even carrying the ticket in my pocket ... If I had been able to catch up with that powerful Mercedes I would have offered them my seat ... I've always liked Carlos Fuentes; not in vain had I chosen him for my experiment. I felt like a scoundrel. Everything that was happening was my fault, and now, instead of putting everything on the line to rid the world of this threat (it was the least I could do), I was allowing myself to be carried away by a private, sentimental whim; I was ashamed of my lack of responsibility.

To appease my conscience, I said out loud, "It will take us only a few minutes. Then all three of us will go to the mountain."

She indicated where to turn and continued directing me along a sinuous route. She leaned forward and pointed her finger in the direction I should go. I couldn't avoid looking at her, and I seemed to be seeing her, again, for the first time. Again I discovered her beauty, her youth ... a bit excessive for me, but that's what it was all about. To be young again, "good and beautiful," as she had said. She was mysterious, that little Nelly, her serenity and silence shielded some kind of secret that enthralled me ...

Here there is a blank in the story. I don't know what happened in the following few minutes. Perhaps we never reached Amelina's place, perhaps we got there and didn't find her, or couldn't rouse her. What I do know is that I suddenly found myself about a hundred feet below street level on the banks of a stream through a deep gorge that crosses the valley and the city longitudinally. Behind me, far above, was the viaduct, the most centrally located bridge connecting the two sides of the gorge. A large crowd had gathered on the other side and was watching me. In front of me, almost perfectly still, was a worm. He was little more than fifty feet away. Apparently the monster had rolled there: his descent had been brutal, judging from what he had left in his wake: fallen trees, houses smashed to smithereens. His congeners must have been surrounding the city in a deadly grip. I looked around. The balconies of the buildings along the edge of the gorge were full of people, eager to witness the confrontation. I recognized the Nancy Building, whose pinkish walls emitted an opaque hue that tinged everybody with their color.

But I had to hurry. The sense of urgency was the only thing that had survived my amnesia. My hands were clutching the vertical bars of the Exoscope, and Nelly was holding the other end. I saw her through the glass panels. How had we gotten there, and with that device? I didn't have time to reconstruct it all, but I could imagine it. Upon seeing the worm fall into the deep riverbed, the lowest level it could reach, I must have thought it would be at my mercy, at least for a few minutes, so I could test an annihilation experiment. We probably ran to the plaza, several hundred feet away, to get the Exoscope, then carried it (this was evident from how every muscle in my body ached) and lowered it from the viaduct: the rope still attached to it was testimony enough.

Whatever the nature of the experiment, I didn't even have to think about it because my brain, in parallel, was already making the calculations ...

"A little more ... here ... slowly ..."

Poor Nelly was panting from the effort. We stood the Exoscope up in front of the worm and carefully turned the glass panels. A fraction of an inch in either direction would make all the difference. I saw the worm's reflection and touched its image in the cold glass with the tips of my fingers. Though threatening, brutal, as lethal as a soft skyscraper come to life, it was beautiful, a masterpiece. I am fascinated by what is huge, excessive. Perhaps never before had such a creature trodden upon the earth, a being made of blue silk, so artificial and at the same time so natural. All its fascination resided in its magnification. It was still a miniature, on which the limitless freedom of size had operated.

I turned to look at it directly. It had moved closer. Though it had no face, it had a vague expressiveness that seemed to speak of its horror at having been born, its feeling of not being welcome, of having landed where it wasn't wanted. I could have stayed there for hours contemplating it. After all, I had good reason to believe it to be my masterpiece. I would never again create anything like it, even if I wanted to. What gave it that particular blue hue was the depth of its materiality, the fact that each cell was composed of reality and unreality. As if my gaze were stimulating it, it began to move, though most likely it had never stopped moving. It covered the distance between us with what was probably, for it, no more than a shudder. Nelly took refuge behind me; the audience held its breath. I lifted my eyes to its formidable mass—the height of a five-story building. It was now or never.

Just as it was supposed to happen, at that instant a ray of sun shone through a break in the mountains and in a straight line onto the glass of the Exoscope. I expertly moved the panels so that the yellow point would draw a tiny square. I knew well the effect this action of the light would have on the cloned cells. And, indeed, the worm began to get reabsorbed into its own reflection in the glass. It was very quick, very fluid, but it was not without incident. The structure of the Exoscope shook, and I was afraid it would fall over. I held one end with all my strength and asked Nelly to do the same on the other. She obeyed me, in spite of her fear. It seemed as if it were going to break apart, but we held firm, and the worm kept going and going ... When less than a tenth of its mass was still materialized, it coiled up around us. I closed my eyes. I felt it slipping, almost brushing up against me, and the blue color penetrated me even through my lowered eyelids. When I lifted those lids, it had finished its reentry ... Or, rather, it hadn't. One last fragment of blue substance remained, which, perhaps because it was the last, rose up in a violent whirlwind on Nelly's end then quickly got sucked into the glass. The movement made one of her shoes fly off, and I saw that her foot was wounded.

The Exoscope was still. I leaned over to look into the glass. There it was, a transparent blue phylactery dissolving into atoms and mixing up with the golden atoms of the sun in a furious battle, in an inoffensive, artistic game that dispersed in seconds. But one drop of blood on Nelly's foot had splashed onto the glass. In a swish, the atomic beam carried it away into the depth of the transparency.

I stood back. It was over. The audience applauded and cheered, joyous honking began to resound throughout the city. The entire herd of gigantic worms had disappeared, dissolved into the dawn air. People took it as some kind of miracle, but I, of course, knew that clones were like that: one is all.

I examined my friend's foot, which was bleeding profusely. Men and boys were climbing down the gorge, and the first to arrive offered to carry her up; the wound wasn't serious, but she needed to be taken to the emergency room to be bandaged. I climbed up behind them, and when they'd gotten her into the car, I told her that I was leaving on the morning flight, as planned. She promised to come to the airport to say goodbye.

MARCH 8, 1996

César Aira

"Once you start reading Aira, you don't want to stop."
  —Roberto Bolaño

"His brutal humor and off-kilter sense of beauty make his stories slip down like spiked cream puffs."
  —Natasha Wimmer, *The New York Times*

"Aira is firmly in the tradition of Jorge Luis Borges and W. G. Sebald, those great late modernists for whom fiction was a theater of ideas."   —Mark Doty, *Los Angeles Times*

"César Aira's body of work is a perfect machine for invention—he writes without necessity or any apparent forebears, always as if for the first time."   —María Moreno, *Bomb*

César Aira was born in Coronel Pringles, Argentina in 1949, and has lived in Buenos Aires since 1967. He taught at the University of Buenos Aires (on Copi and Rimbaud) and at the University of Rosario (Constructivism and Mallarmé), and has translated and edited books from France, England, Italy, Brazil, Spain, Mexico, and Venezuela. He is one of the most prolific writers in Argentina, having published more than sixty books to date.